To Bri

With best wishes.

T. C. Lawrence

FATAL PARADISE